A TREASURY OF Welsh Heroes

illustrations by
Brett Breckon

Pont

A TREASURY OF
Welsh Heroes

Contents

Saint David

It's a lovely spring morning in Glyn Rhosyn. Everything's quiet, hardly a sound, just the swish-swash of the sea lapping the shore, and a wave breaking against the rocks every now and then. We aren't expecting any visitors, though the sea can make this a busy place, with boats and coracles coming to us from as far away as Gwynedd and Ireland and sometimes as far as Brittany. But as I look towards the horizon today, there's no sign of anything coming in our direction. I'm hoping that the community here will get some peace so that we can carry on with our work and prayers.

Last Tuesday an important messenger came to visit me and told me I should prepare a very special sermon. It's one that I'm going to preach in our next public mass. And I need time to prepare it carefully.

Yes, everything is quiet today, though you'd hardly believe how exciting things can be here sometimes. I remember once how an Irish monk, Scuthyn, came to warn me that there were traitors in Glyn Rhosyn. I was so grateful to my friend Aeddan. God had told him about the conspiracy and he arranged for Scuthyn, poor soul, to come all the way by sea from Ireland to save me. I couldn't imagine that anyone wanted to kill me – I didn't want to believe that I had any enemies in the church.

When one of the conspirators brought a loaf of bread to my table, I broke the bread into three pieces. I gave the first piece to one of our dogs. It dropped dead instantly. I gave the next piece to a crow sitting in a tree next to the church. The bird had only to touch the bread with its beak, and it died right there in front of me. I should have been afraid but I wasn't. I took the third piece of bread and blessed it, and then ate

6

it slowly in front of everyone. I knew that God would take care of me. Then those who'd planned to betray me realised how wrong they'd been, and I forgave them.

I remember another occasion when I had to invite all the monks and priests in Wales to come to a meeting at Llanddewibrefi. The journey there was a bit of an ordeal. Along the way, a woman came up to me; she was sobbing uncontrollably. Quite overcome with grief, she told me that her son had died. I asked her to take me to him, and I was so pleased when I was able to bring him back to life and health again. He awoke from a deep, deep sleep and then he smiled at his mother. I wonder what became of him? Perhaps he grew up to be a fisherman, like his father.

When I got to Llanddewibrefi at last, I was surprised to see how many people had arrived for the meeting. There were representatives from all over Wales, from every church and every parish, and it was difficult to get everyone's attention. I had to speak very, very loudly. I had an important message, and I wanted to make sure that they could all hear me. My message, very simply, was that everyone in Wales should come together and follow the Lord Jesus Christ.

· SAINT DAVID ·

I'm quite a tall man, but nevertheless it was very difficult for everybody to see me. And do you know what? The most amazing thing happened: the ground rose up under my feet – a sure sign that God wanted to help me spread his word – and then a dove came to perch on my shoulder. I was so heartened. That same dove has come to me on a number of occasions and it always brings me comfort. This time it gave me strength to speak out with power and authority, which was vital to the success of the meeting. Each day in my prayers I thank God for raising the ground and for sending the dove to reassure me. And I need God's help more than ever at this moment: the sermon I'm writing is so important . . .

It's strange to think that although I was brought up in the lap of luxury (my father and his forefathers were kings of Ceredigion), I don't miss any of those trappings now. No, I much prefer my life in the monastery, living simply with my fellow monks, eating a plain diet of fruit and vegetables, and drinking water, plenty of water. I don't need meat, fancy wines or mead to make me happy. I take after my mother in that way: she preferred simple food.

My mother was Non, the daughter of Cynyr from Caer Gawch, one of the people who came over to Wales from Ireland. I often think that being of mixed race is a great advantage to me. Because I have the blood of more than one nation flowing through my veins, I can see how stupid it is to make an enemy of someone just because they happen to come from a different country. We must learn to live in peace with one another and remind ourselves that we are all brothers and sisters.

My mother grew up in Henfynyw, near Aberaeron. The people in that area

9

adored her. They even named a church after her at Llan-non, near Henfynyw, and they built another in her honour at Llannerch Aeron. In later life she became a nun and did a lot to help the poor and needy.

The area around Aberaeron is truly amazing: you can see all the way from Glyn Rhosyn in Pembrokeshire right up to the Llŷn peninsula and, on a clear day, you can even see as far as Ireland. But although Aberaeron is beautiful, I must admit that Glyn Rhosyn is the place I call home. It was close to here that I was born, one wild and stormy night. According to my mother, an enormous stone split and landed by her foot when she gave birth to me and, at the same moment, a spring gushed from the rock. That was a wonderful thing to happen. Fresh water is scarce and finding a new spring gives people hope and life.

This is a very special part of the world. The early Celtic druids settled here, and then Saint Patrick came over from Ireland to explain more about the teachings of Jesus. Patrick established a community of Christians. He was Irish, and quite a large number of Irish people have come to this area. There's a hill we call Boia's Peak, Clegyr Boia, where a very different kind of Irishman lived. He wasn't at all like Saint Patrick: in fact he was a bit of a pirate. Poor Boia. He wasn't very happy when I first came here to live. But after we talked together, we became quite close friends and eventually he asked me to baptise him in the river Alun. He had taken the words of Jesus to his heart.

Unfortunately Boia's wife wasn't very happy about this. She tried everything to cause trouble for our community. She was determined to take our minds away from our prayers, and even sent beautiful dancing girls one night to distract us – though she

10

didn't succeed and neither did they! We have dedicated our lives to Jesus and nothing is going to change our minds. But she was so angry! It's hard to imagine how anyone could be that angry. Eventually, in a fit of rage, she cut the throat of her stepdaughter, Dunawd! At once a miracle happened and a healing spring began to flow from the very spot where the poor girl's blood had been spilt. But that wasn't the end of the violence. The same terrible night that Dunawd was murdered, a huge fire raged through the castle at Clegyr Boia. It had been started by another wild-tempered Irishman who lived in the area. His name was Lisci and he stabbed my friend Boia to death.

Imagine the scene: the storm, the screaming, the raging fire, the spilt blood. Yes, it's hard to believe on a quiet spring morning like today, isn't it? Two wells mark these sad events – Ffynnon Llygad (the waters are said to help with eye problems) and Ffynnon Clegyr Boia. I'm afraid we've got a very long way to go before we learn Jesus's lessons about living at peace with one other.

As I look back on my life, I realise how lucky I've been. Not many people are able to read and write, but I had the chance to learn both of those skills. I had an excellent teacher called Paulinus, who was master of his craft; I used to go to him at Llanddeusant. It doesn't matter how much I practise, though: I know very well that I won't ever be able to write as neatly as Paulinus. He used his pen like an artist and, although he was blind, every letter on every page was perfectly formed.

One of the happiest days of my life was when I cured his blindness by laying my hands upon his eyes. I hoped – no, I was sure – that I could help him to see again. Through God's grace I knew I'd be able to lift the veil from his old eyes. I'll never

forget that day. He began reciting his favourite psalm: 'I will lift up mine eyes unto the hills . . .', his voice ringing with gratitude. I think that's the day I decided that I wanted to become a monk, like Paulinus. Something deep inside told me that it was the right thing to do.

At the beginning, maybe, I hadn't realised quite how hard a monk's life would be. You need strong muscles and a lot of staying power. One of our most difficult tasks is ploughing by hand. We have to drag the plough across rough, stony ground – with no oxen to help us – and for that we need strong arms. But at harvest time, after the spring rain has watered the ground, and the warm summer sun has coaxed the oats from the soil, the sight of the dancing, golden fields makes me realise how wonderful God is. As long as we work together and care for the land God gave us, it will supply everything we need.

It's not just working on the land that's hard. Building is quite a business too. Not that we monks build very grand houses like those of princes and kings. But even for a very simple building like ours, we needed a lot of muscle power.

A number of monks have come to join our community at Glyn Rhosyn, and some of them are my pupils. I'm sure I'm not as good a teacher as Paulinus, but I try my best. They have started calling the place 'Tyddewi', or 'St David's'. The name makes me smile! One monk says that he predicts that one day there will be more than sixty places across Wales named after me! Well, I don't mind what people call their villages, so long as they help one another to follow the teaching of Jesus.

I know from experience how difficult that can be. As I've already said, I've seen

bitter quarrels, fierce fighting and bloodshed. The loss of life, sometimes. These days there is far too much fighting. Fighting against the Irish in the west of the country. Fighting against the English in the east. And fighting amongst ourselves too – family against family, tribe against tribe.

Perhaps it's not surprising that more and more people are turning their backs on such cruel ways. I've heard that all over the world, from Egypt to Asia, from Spain and France to the Netherlands, people are choosing to live their lives as I do. What could be better for a life of prayer than the peace and quiet of a monk's cell? And if others decide to join us at Glyn Rhosyn, all well and good, so long as they respect the silence that we need to worship God.

I think that my favourite work here is collecting honey from the bees and gathering the roots of plants to make healing medicines. God has given us everything we need to live a healthy life and, if we sometimes become ill, he has put the cure into our own hands – so long as we help one another. Sometimes, just doing the smallest thing can bring a smile to the face of a friend. And smiling makes everyone feel better, doesn't it?

People around here are scared of illness – and no wonder! Less than half a century ago they were struck by a terrible plague – yellow fever – which killed hundreds of people. Whole families were wiped out, along with their animals. But, thanks be to God, everybody looks healthy now, and there are animals grazing in the fields once more.

After early prayers each day, when the sun is beginning to warm the earth, we go out to the fields to work. Then, after we've laboured all morning and for part of the afternoon, we come back and sit together to read and write. Some of us visit people

13

in the local neighbourhood, dispensing medicine and food where they're needed. But when the church bell rings, whatever we're doing, we come together and pray until the stars begin to appear. Sometimes we chant psalms. I often think that the stars enjoy listening to our chanting and take it as their signal to venture out into the night sky.

At supper-time there's enough food for everyone, though never too much. And after we've finished eating, we gather together once more for an evening service of three hours or so before returning to our cells to sleep.

No, I don't think this life would suit everyone!

Sometimes before settling down to sleep, I stand in cold water. Somehow the cold helps me to forget about my body and allows me to concentrate entirely on God. And that's what I'm doing now. Concentrating and asking God to help me with my sermon. I already know what my closing words will be: 'Brothers and sisters, rejoice and keep the faith, and do the little things.'

Yes, and that really will be the end. Not just the end of my preaching, but the end of my life too. Because the messenger who told me to prepare my sermon was an angel. He told me that I will die on the first day of March in the year 589. That's only a week away and it's why I need to make sure that this sermon says everything. It's my very last chance.

Rhodri Mawr

. . .

Everybody has a name. It's one of the first things we're given when we're born. Your parents will have given you a name, maybe Daniel or Jack, Hannah or Helen. But you will also have another name, your surname. That's your family name, like Jones or Evans or Williams. In Wales, many years ago, things were different. You had your own name, then *ap* and then your father's name. Take Huw ap Siôn. *Ap* means son: so the whole thing means Huw, son of Siôn. If you were a girl, you would have *ach* instead of *ap*. Dafydd's daughter Gwenllïan would be called Gwenllïan ach Dafydd. But sometimes even the Welsh would break with their own tradition and use a second name which actually described the person it belonged to.

Just imagine this happening today. What would your second name be? How would you describe yourself? Steffan the sporty? Wendy the wise? Cai the calm? Bethan the bold? The name of one Welsh princess was Elen Luyddog. This meant that she had many servants and people prepared to defend her. What a lovely name to have! But just imagine if you were called Davy Gam. *Gam* means crooked. So, did that mean that Davy Gam was a crook?

One of the most famous people to have this kind of name was a king, Rhodri, who ruled in Wales in the ninth century. That's about 1200 years ago! He was the first Welsh ruler to earn the name 'Great'. There have been several others since. Perhaps you've heard of Llywelyn the Great?

Today children often take after their parents in the kind of work they do. What do your parents do? Would you like to follow in their footsteps? Sometimes the children

of doctors also grow up to be doctors, the children of plumbers often become plumbers, and the children of rugby players grow up to play rugby. Rhodri came from a family of kings. His father was a king, so it was natural for Rhodri to become a king too. His father was called Merfyn and his mother was called Nest. Merfyn was king of the Isle of Man, the island in the middle of the sea between Wales, Ireland and Scotland. After winning a battle in Gwynedd, north Wales, Merfyn became king there too, and that is how Rhodri grew up to become king of Gwynedd.

He was born around the year 820. There are no pictures of him, of course. Cameras hadn't been invented in those days. And if anyone ever painted his portrait or did a pen-and-ink sketch, then it's long since vanished. The only information we have about Rhodri is a few sentences written about him at the time, and our imaginations, of course! We have to imagine a pretty special sort of person. He must have been unusual to earn the name Rhodri Mawr, Rhodri the Great, rather than Rhodri ap Merfyn.

It's certain that he had a comfortable upbringing. As the king's son, he did not go short of food. He was probably taught how to hunt and how to use a bow and arrow when he was very young. He must also have had to live under the threat of attack from enemies throughout his life. Imagine if every night you went to sleep you had to worry about whether or not the country next door was going to attack you or burn down your village. It's good to know that these days we can go to bed happily without having to worry about things like that. Wouldn't it be wonderful if that was true of every part of the world?

When Rhodri was twenty-four years old, his father was killed in battle.

When that happened, the king's son immediately became king. Even though he would have been very sad after losing his father, Rhodri's first responsibility was to make sure that enemies beyond the borders of his kingdom did not try and invade.

Rhodri fell in love with a girl called Angharad. She came from the south, from an area known as Seisyllwg. This tongue-twister of a name isn't used any more, but if you look on a map to find Carmarthenshire and Ceredigion, that's more or less the area which was known as Seisyllwg.

Rhodri wasn't the kind of king to take other people's lands by force. Only bad kings do things like that. But he certainly wanted to defend his own people and their land. One of his bloodiest battles was against the Vikings. They had come across the sea from countries like Denmark, Norway and Sweden. They had fought successfully in England and Scotland and decided that they'd like to come to Wales as well.

But they didn't know that Wales already had a king, and a brave one too, who was determined to stop them. That king was Rhodri.

The Vikings had set their sights on invading Anglesey. There aren't many hills or mountains on the island, so you'd think that it would be easy for an invading army to come ashore and kill the inhabitants. But Rhodri the Great was ready for the invaders.

There were rich churches and monasteries on the island at that time and the Vikings would have liked nothing better than to raid the religious buildings, burn them to the ground and steal all the treasure. During the battle, however, they realised that they were going to lose and that Rhodri's troops were too strong and too clever for them. And so the Vikings fled back to England.

Just imagine if Rhodri had lost the battle. The people of Anglesey might be speaking Danish or Norwegian today rather than Welsh or English.

Rhodri's mother came from Powys and her brother, Cyngen ap Cadell, was the ruler there. When Cyngen died in the year 855, Rhodri the Great became king of Powys. He must have been a good king and leader, as so many people were willing to be ruled by him.

People liked both Rhodri and his wife, Angharad. They defended the people of Powys and Gwynedd and made sure that nobody attacked or killed them. In the year 871 Angharad's brother Gwgon, the king of Seisyllwg, was out at sea when there was a terrible storm, during which everyone on the boat was killed. Gwgon didn't have any children and so his people had to find a new king. And that is how Rhodri took charge of Seisyllwg too. Angharad was pleased that her husband and her sons would rule the land where she was born and grew up. More importantly, the people of Seisyllwg were happy because they knew that Rhodri was a kind and fair king. So, Rhodri now ruled most of Wales, from Anglesey in the north to the area around present-day Swansea.

He wanted to make sure that nobody could attack his land and, because he had so much territory by this time, defending it was becoming more and more difficult. And so he decided to build a new castle. Rhodri travelled the length and breadth of the country to find the best place to build it. He went to Aberystwyth, Cardigan, Carmarthen, Swansea and many other places. These locations were all good, but when he arrived in one particular place, he knew that this was the perfect site for his castle. It was called Dinefwr, near to modern-day Llandeilo. It was a good site with a steep hill and a gentle river flowing past. The land all around was rich and fertile. Rhodri's people would be able to grow plenty of food. 'This is the place,' he thought, and proceeded to build a castle there.

Rhodri the Great must have chosen a 'great' place to build his castle, because if you go to Dinefwr, you can still see it. Rhodri's castle was probably built of wood but the one we visit today is built of stone. The people who came after him could see the same advantages as he did. This really was a great place for a castle.

In the year 877 when Rhodri had only been king of Seisyllwg for about six years the English decided to attack his borderlands. Because he didn't want to give up territory to the invaders, Rhodri knew that he'd have to defend his kingdom once again, and so he went with his son, Gwriad, to Powys. Nobody knows exactly where the battle took place but, fighting against the English, somewhere in Powys, Rhodri and his son were killed.

Even though they lost their lives, other sons were left, including Anarawd, Cadell and Merfyn, and Rhodri the Great became the grandfather of another wise and brave leader, Hywel Dda. So, Rhodri's family remained in power in Wales for very many years after his death. He was the first king to unite most of Wales from north to south. For centuries after that, every king and prince tried to do the same, and ensure that Wales was ruled by the Welsh, and nobody else!

Hywel Dda

For the last few weeks we've been buzzing with excitement. Everyone's been sorting, tidying and titivating. Mam and Dad have been much too busy to take any notice of me, and that suits me fine!

As soon as I've snatched a bit of bread for my breakfast, I run out of the cottage behind the forge and climb trees or hide in the bushes until it's time for bed. I spend the whole day watching everybody else hard at work. Dad's a blacksmith, and he's been busy shoeing horses, and making all sorts of tools to help the farmers tend their fields. You should see the sparks fly when his blacksmith's hammer hits the white-hot metal after it's just come out of the fire! Migildi-magildi-hey-now-NOW! That's the rhythm of the hammering – tap-a-tap, tap-a-tap . . . tap . . . tap . . . TAP. Several smaller blows and then one final crash!

Do you know why there's so much fuss? It's because King Hywel is coming home! From time to time he likes to come back here to hunt, but nobody's seen him in these parts for a very long while. He has been away on his travels for so long, meeting the king of Wessex in England, and setting the whole kingdom of Wales to rights, from Prestatyn in the north to Pembrokeshire in the south.

There's a rumour that he's even travelled as far as Rome, on a pilgrimage to visit the Pope! Anyway, he's on his way here now to hold an important meeting, and everybody wants to put on a good show. You should see the women. They're rushed off their feet, scrubbing and cleaning, painting walls and preparing all sorts of dainties and delicacies to eat. The men are busy too, doing repairs outdoors and turning over the soil in the reeve's garden.

28

Today I managed to hide in the waggon as my big brother Dafydd was driving a cartload of wool. He was taking it over to the building where the meeting will be held. I nearly got caught! Dafydd was grumbling and sweating and complaining because the load was heavier than he expected. Thank goodness, I realised in the nick of time that he was about to come and find out why the wool was so heavy. Just before we got to the reeve's land, I managed to jump out. Then I ran along the hedgerow all the way to the big house.

You should see the reeve's garden! It's amazing! Everything grows there. Vegetables and herbs and flowers. When summer comes there'll be so much nectar that the bees will be buzzing for joy – and there'll be loads of honey. The air smells of fresh gorse and heather. And excitement, of course. Everybody's working flat out.

Yesterday we had a message to say that Hywel would be arriving this morning and that he's bringing a dozen important people with him. He wants to put our legal system into some kind of order. They say that he's going to find out how things are done in different parts of Wales. He wants to work out what's fair, to make sure that all the people of Wales, north and south, are treated equally. He and his advisors are going to decide on the best system. And then, wherever in Wales people live, they will know how to behave. The same laws will apply to everybody. The grown-ups all think that this is a very good idea. Me? I just can't wait to see all the grand folk arriving!

At first I couldn't work out what the noise was. I wondered if it was my heart, beating very loudly. Then I thought it might be a thunderstorm on the way. That idea really scared me, hiding up in the tree, but I was too frightened to come down. I wished that I'd done as I was told and stayed near the smithy where Dad could keep an eye on me.

And then I realised that it wasn't thunder. And no one's heart beats that loudly!

What I could hear was the sound of horses' hooves. They were getting closer. Really close! And mounted on each horse was a fine gentleman wearing brightly coloured clothes. The important folk had arrived. And yes! That first horseman had to be King Hywel, Hywel ap Cadell. As he galloped past, I caught a glimpse of his face. It was strong and handsome, but wise too. I wondered what he saw with those piercing eyes. It was if he could see further than anybody else.

I stayed quite still in my hiding place high above the garden until the last of the horses had galloped past. I waited until the dust on the pathway settled again and until the last of the hoof beats died away.

I waited a moment longer, then I slipped down from my tree and ran all the way home with the news. Hywel ap Cadell, high king of Wales, had arrived in Whitland.

Next day I wasn't allowed to go any further than the smithy door. But I was desperate to hear what was happening in the meeting up at the reeve's house. And it was like that for days. Waiting and waiting, hanging around the forge, carrying wood to stoke up the fire so that Dad could melt iron to make horseshoes and tools and weapons.

He must have noticed how restless I was, so by the time the sun was going down on the third day, he told me I could stay up that night, because the king's official bard had promised to call by to tell us all the latest news.

I couldn't believe my luck in being allowed to stay up late. I'd get to hear all about the king's important meeting from no less a person than the royal poet himself. This was going to be a night to remember!

I must have fallen asleep by the fire when he arrived, because I've no memory of seeing him come in. All I can remember is opening my eyes and seeing a long-haired man wearing a cloak. He was sitting opposite me on a three-legged stool and he held a stick and a small harp. His voice was deep and calm. As he recited his words it sounded like music although he wasn't exactly singing. Every now and again he would stop speaking and pull the strings on the harp. Sometimes, when he was reciting, he would strike the floor with his stick until the ground vibrated with the blows. It made me feel as if my whole body was being carried away, like a boat riding the waves.

31

When I opened my eyes the bard was in the middle of recounting the history of Hywel's family. His grandfather was Rhodri the Great, the son of Merfyn and Nest. Merfyn had been king of Gwynedd, and Nest's father was also a king, in Powys. So when Rhodri became king, he ruled Gwynedd. Later on he inherited Powys. Rhodri left three sons, Anarawd, Cadell and Merfyn, and a daughter, Nest. Cadell, who conquered Dyfed, was Hywel's father.

My head was starting to spin with all these names and I nearly went back to sleep. But I understood this much: when Hywel was born to Cadell, he automatically became king of Gwynedd, Powys and Dyfed, and in no time at all, he seems to have taken possession of Ceredigion and Ystrad Tywi in Carmarthenshire. I didn't understand all of it, and it was hard to hear everything with the sound of the fire crackling, but I think the lands of Ceredigion and Ystrad Tywi had a strange-sounding name. It was something very odd, a real tongue-twister like 'Seisyllwg'.

So, imagine! Once more one man was king of all the lands from the Menai Strait in north Wales to the river Tywi in the south. (Not forgetting the river Taf, of course. That's our river, here in Whitland.) And tonight this powerful king, Hywel son of Cadell, was sleeping not a stone's throw from the blacksmith's cottage. He was tucked up in bed in the reeve's house! I decided there and then that I was going to try and get out of the smithy the next day to take a closer look at him.

But back to the story. The bard held the audience spellbound. He said that Hywel was very well educated and that he could speak Welsh – well, that wasn't a big thing, I thought, even I could speak Welsh – but, no, Hywel could also speak English as fluently as the king of Wessex, and Latin too, the language of the Romans, and, yes, it was perfectly true: Hywel had travelled the whole way to Rome. There was one awful story about the time he went there and saw someone being put to death. (But I can't tell you any more, because hearing about it made me feel sick, and I must admit that I put my fingers in my ears so that I couldn't hear any more.)

Because he'd read and travelled and learnt so much, Hywel realised how important it was for us in Wales to govern our country wisely. We had to come to an agreement about the best way of doing things so that we could all live in peace with each other. The fact that Hywel had called everybody together showed that he was a wise and fair leader. After all, in many other countries in Europe, the king decided what laws to make without discussing them with anybody. And, according to the bard, if somebody dared to disagree, they'd get sent straight to jail – if they were lucky! Or hanged, if they weren't.

'Thank you, God, for sending us a good and wise king like Hywel!' the bard announced suddenly. And Mam and Dad said 'Hear, hear!'. I plucked up my courage and said 'Amen' too to show that I agreed, trying to make my voice sound as deep as I could.

At one point, the bard started reciting the names of all the important people who had come to Whitland with Hywel. Hearing him reel off the list of long titles was like being hypnotised. They were all good names but the one I liked best was Bledrws, son of Bleiddyd. Even Gwyn the reeve got a mention because it was in his house that they were holding the meeting.

There were scribes there too, or nobody would have been able to remember what had been agreed. One of the scribes was the archdeacon in the diocese of Llandaff. Three copies of the laws would be written down: one would go to Dinefwr in the south, one to Mathrafal in the middle of the country and one would go to Aberffraw in the north.

There was one thing that made me feel really sorry for the bigwigs. Because we were in the middle of Lent, Hywel decided that everybody had to fast before they could begin on the main task of discussing the laws. *Ych a fi!* Fasting! I know what that means! Not eating – not even a piece of dry bread or the tiniest bit of cheese.

Hywel was sure that everybody would be in a better state to think clearly if they fasted. I wasn't so sure myself; I thought that it would be easier to concentrate with a full stomach.

Anyway, there was no need to feel too sorry for them because, so the bard informed us, they could look forward to a real banquet at the end of each day's discussions. Enough food for all and everybody happy and relaxed after doing so much thinking.

My dad asked whether Hywel had decided that we should have similar laws to the Romans. After all, their laws were world famous. But no! The bard had heard Hywel himself saying, after a lot of deliberation, that the old Welsh laws were a lot fairer than all the Roman ones. My dad smiled and I knew it did his heart good to hear this. For one thing, the old Welsh laws said that the blacksmith was an important man. You had to have permission from the lord of the manor before you could teach your son (or anybody else for that matter) to be a blacksmith, and being a teacher gave you special status. It was the same if you wanted to teach someone to be a scholar or a bard. I really hoped that one day Dad would get permission to teach me to be a blacksmith.

But the bard had moved ahead with his story. You should have heard him explaining the detailed work that went into drawing up all the laws. There was a law for everybody and everything. A law for the king and queen, the priest, the servant, the maid and the doctor. There was even a law for the bard. I thought that this was starting to sound like a total hotchpotch, but the grown-ups all agreed that life would be much easier from now on, with everybody knowing exactly what their rights were and what the punishment would be for breaking the law.

I didn't like the sound of that word 'punishment'. I remembered only too well getting a clout from my dad for stealing an apple from the orchard in Tŷ Gwyn last summer, and I didn't want another one. Not if I could help it!

And while I was thinking about this, I thought again about my idea for getting out of the smithy the following morning. I'd now listened to so much about good behaviour, I decided instead that I'd better ask Dad for his permission. Maybe he'd let me go or, even better, maybe he'd be willing to come with me.

Next day Dad and I went for a walk to the reeve's house. The maid, Elin, who was a friend of Mam's, gave us a big welcome in the kitchen. And when it was supper-time, Elin allowed me – yes me! – to carry a dish full of fruit into the big room so that I could get a closer look at all the gentlemen. They were sitting around a large table,

35

and in the middle there were lots of documents of various kinds. In the corner one man was using a quill to write carefully onto a beautiful manuscript.

There was no need to ask which one Hywel was. I noticed him straight away. He was sitting on a large throne. He looked slightly different to the others. He wore the same sort of clothes, and he had the same style of hair, but there was something in his eyes, that same look I'd noticed when he rode past. That's probably what makes you a good leader, I thought, when you can see further than everyone else.

But all that was a long, long time ago. These days I'm the blacksmith, although I'm getting on a bit now. My mam and dad died many years ago. I'm glad to say I was given permission to teach my son the blacksmith's craft, and now he's the one operating the big hammer. It's the same old rhythm though. Migildi-magildi-hey-now-NOW! And when night draws in, and the smithy grows quiet, I love to tell my son and grandson all about Hywel ap Cadell. They like listening to the stories, especially my little grandson because he's called Hywel too! The part he likes best is where Hywel is given the name Hywel Dda, Hywel the Good . . . because, between you and me and the gatepost, young Hywel isn't always a good boy – he likes to climb trees and hide out in his big brother's cart. But there we are! I can't say much about that, can I?

There's just one last thing I want to tell you. It's about some words which were inscribed on a beautiful scroll after Hywel Dda's death: 'In the Year of Our Lord 948,

Hywel Dda died. Son of Cadell, King of Wales, he was the wisest and the most righteous of all princes. He loved peace and justice, and feared God. He governed conscientiously, righteously and peacefully. He was much beloved by everybody, both by the people of Wales, and by wise men from England and from other countries, and, because of that, he was named Hywel Dda, Hywel the Good.'

What a pity that he left four sons, Owain, Rhun, Rhodri and Edwyn, who fell out amongst themselves and fought each other. Not one of them possessed the gift of long sight, and many years passed before Hywel Dda's well-governed kingdom could once more live in peace.

Princess Nest

. . .

n the banks of the Teifi river
In a beautiful tree-lined valley,
There stands a castle newly built
Which tells an old, old story.

It's the tale of a beautiful princess,
The loveliest ever seen,
And her story is whispered amongst the leaves
That shadow the Teifi stream.

From the hour of her birth, Nest was beautiful,
The daughter of Rhys ap Tudor,
And one day in all her loveliness
The bold King Henry viewed her.

He brought her to live in London town
Where she bore the king a son,
But later the lovely Princess Nest
Returned to Wales alone.

She was given as wife to a nobleman,
She had no say in the matter,
And the name of her jealous husband was
The Norman, Gerald de Windsor.

42

He marvelled at his beautiful wife
(In Wales there was none so fair)
And he built for her a beautiful home,
A castle beyond compare.

Surrounded by a deer park
It had pastures of the best,
The finest deer herd grazed there –
To this day it is called Parc Nest.

But despite the trees and the river
The beautiful princess was sad,
Green fields and hills were not enough
To make her spirits glad.

Her heart ached with such sadness
That she wept all day and all night
For she'd never known a moment's love,
Oh, pity her lonely plight!

Until Owain ap Cadogan
Arrived at the castle one day,
And he soon became her closest friend
And chased her tears away.

· PRINCESS NEST ·

Nest fled from the mighty castle
Within his protecting arm,
For Owain had sworn to defend his love
And deliver her free from harm.

But Gerald, whose jealous nature
Could not bear that his wife should depart,
Drew his cruel sword upon Owain
And pierced him through the heart.

When Nest heard of his murder
Her tears began to flow,
She fell to the floor in her misery,
Cast down by grief and woe.

And if you go for a riverside stroll
In Newcastle Emlyn's meadow,
You might just hear Nest calling yet
From the depths of her lonely sorrow.

If only you could have seen Angharad, wife of the king of Gwynedd! In the whole of Wales there was no one more beautiful. Her hair shone like burnished gold and her eyes were wide and sparkling. She was graceful and dignified in her speech and in the way she moved. She was always kind and always ready to do someone a good turn. No woman was ever as perfect as Angharad – apart, that is, from her own daughter, Gwenllïan.

Gwenllïan was the youngest in the family, and she was a favourite with her older brothers and sisters, as well as with her parents. She was always smiling, and somehow she had the knack of making everybody around her smile too. As she grew up, her beauty increased, so it's hardly surprising that a lot of young men in Wales wanted to marry her. But Gwenllïan wasn't planning on marrying anybody in a hurry. She wanted to be absolutely sure that she loved her future husband. She would rather not get married at all and be a nun than have to share her life with somebody she didn't love.

At that time, around the year 1100, Wales was a very dangerous place, under attack from wave after wave of foreign invaders. Men from Flanders (modern Belgium) and Normandy, as well as England, were eager to get their hands on a piece of Wales. There had been a lot of trouble in the south, in the Dinefwr area, until finally, Gruffudd ap Rhys, the prince of that region, had to make a run for it. With the Normans hot on his heels, he took refuge in north Wales, in Gwynedd.

Whilst he was in hiding in the north, Gruffudd became friends with Gwenllïan. Well, actually, they became more than just friends, and within no time at all they

48

were very much in love. Gruffudd knew in his heart that he would never meet anybody as beautiful or good-natured as Gwenllïan, and she knew that she would never meet anybody as handsome or loving as Gruffudd. She was sure that he was the man for her. She was either going to marry Gruffudd ap Rhys from Dinefwr or nobody at all!

One still night, when the sea was quiet and a ship lay at anchor, ready to take the young prince back to fight for his kingdom in the south, Gruffudd and Gwenllïan agreed to get married as soon as they possibly could. They were both very happy. They were sure that they would be able to face any hardship together, even in a country torn by fear and hatred. More than anything they hoped to be able to bring peace to Wales.

As well as being beautiful and wise, Gwenllïan was also brave. She didn't want to wait until Gruffudd won his kingdom back before getting married; after all, there was no knowing when that would happen. No, she wasn't afraid! In any case – whatever the danger – she wanted to be with Gruffudd more than anything in the world. Gwenllïan thought there was probably more danger of her dying of grief in her father's home on Anglesey than losing her life in an enemy attack in the south. So, one night, against her family's advice, she decided to leave the safety of her father's court in Gwynedd and follow Gruffudd back to Dinefwr. Her sisters, Mared, Rhiannell, Susanna and Annest, and her brothers, Cadwallon, Owain and Cadwaladr, all came to say goodbye. Even though it was hard to leave her family behind, Gwenllïan was certain that Dinefwr was the place she wanted to be.

Gruffudd could hardly believe his eyes when he saw Gwenllïan coming towards him. She wore a long blue gown and she looked so beautiful. Without a moment's delay, but quietly so as not to attract the enemy's attention, the two young people made for the heart of the forest of Ystrad Tywi. And there they were married. There weren't many guests, just a few close friends. There was no grand ceremony, no wedding feast, and no royal celebration, just a chorus of birdsong and a fluttering of leaves as they made their marriage vows.

In time, all the people of the local area came to love Gwenllïan. She was so cheerful and pleasant, always ready to help anybody, and she was never downhearted. Her smiles and kind words made everybody feel better. The Welsh people even began to dream that they might once again live in peace. Wherever Gwenllïan went, she gave them hope.

The court at Dinefwr quickly gained a reputation for being a warm and loving home,

50

full of the sound of children's laughter. Gruffudd and Gwenllïan were very fond of their children and were amazed at how quickly they grew. Morgan was the eldest, Maelgwyn was the middle child, and Rhys was the little one, the baby of the family.

But although their home was a happy one, a shadow hung over the court at Dinefwr. It was a dangerous place to live. Sometimes, if the threat from the enemy was very serious, the entire household had to flee the palace and make for the mountains and the forests. When this happened, the children had to be brave and daring, just like their parents. They quite enjoyed their night-time adventures escaping from the enemy. They would all huddle close together and, before snuggling up to sleep under a warm blanket, they would listen to the court poet, or bard, reciting stories and ballads about brave Welshmen and women. Little Rhys, especially, liked to hear the poems and the singing.

Gwenllïan was always worried that one day the enemy might find them and hurt one of her children. But she never showed what she was feeling.

In 1136, when Gwenllïan was nearly forty years old, her husband decided the time had come to join forces with his father-in-law, Gruffudd ap Cynan of Gwynedd. Together they could put a stop to the Normans and the English, who were set on taking more and more Welsh land. Another prince, Hywel of Brycheiniog, had defeated the invaders in a battle at Loughor, near Swansea. This gave hope to the Dinefwr family. If Hywel had succeeded, maybe, by joining forces, the Welsh could beat the enemy once and for all.

'I will go and ask your father for help, Gwenllïan,' Gruffudd announced, 'because one thing's for sure. We're going to have to work together if we're going to defeat the enemy!'

'You're right,' Gwenllïan said. 'You go, and I'll take care of the children and defend Dinefwr. I have fought alongside you many times now. I am as strong as any man, and I have enough authority to command an army.'

'God keep you safe,' Gruffudd replied. 'Wait for me. I will return as soon as possible. Maybe, when I come back, there will be no enemy left to terrorise this country of ours.'

'Let's hope so,' said Gwenllïan. 'But you will take great care, won't you?' She didn't want to show her husband how upset she was. Although she'd have the children for company, she knew how much she was going to miss him.

They kissed goodbye, not knowing that this would be the last time they would see each other . . . Soon after Gruffudd left, a messenger arrived with terrible news. Gwenllïan was shocked to hear that a Norman army had landed in Glamorgan and thousands of soldiers were marching towards the castle at Kidwelly. Gwenllïan knew that she had not a moment to lose.

At that time, Maurice de Londres was the keeper of Kidwelly Castle. He was a man with a really bad reputation. He wanted to capture as much land as he could to increase his personal power. He would have liked nothing better than to own the beautiful palace at Dinefwr and all of the rich farmland in the Tywi valley. It was his ambition to be able to sail the river, go hunting in the hills and boast that all the land was his. He'd had enough of that puffed-up Welshman Gruffudd ap Rhys!

(Maurice didn't want to admit that he was jealous of his rival at Dinefwr, not just because the prince owned such rich and fertile land, but because he was married to such a beautiful wife.)

Gwenllïan knew that she had to act quickly and that it was out of the question to wait for her husband to come back and protect her. She realised that she, her family, and the entire community were in great danger, and that she was the one who would have to take action. Luckily Gwenllïan was both brave and decisive. Immediately she called together all of the chiefs in the area. Between them they agreed on a plan of campaign. They were good fighters and loyal to Gwenllïan and ready to follow her to the battlefield.

First of all she led a small army to keep watch on Kidwelly Castle, and then sent another army, a bigger one, to go and deal with the Norman soldiers who had just landed. She commanded her army to do whatever was necessary to stop the Normans from getting to Kidwelly.

From her hiding place at the foot of Mynydd-y-garreg, Gwenllïan could keep an eye on Kidwelly Castle and on the movements of Maurice de Londres. She would make sure that the wicked old fox couldn't leave his castle to join up with the new forces. And if Maurice and his men decided to attack her, well, they would have to cross the raging Gwendraeth river to do so.

That night, Gwenllïan's heart beat rapidly as she listened to the wind singing its melancholy song in the trees. In spite of everything, she felt confident that she would be able to protect her people. She was determined to make her husband proud

of her and she knew that she must keep the children safe. The two eldest boys, Morgan and Maelgwyn, stayed with their mother. Although they were still very young, Gwenllïan knew that they had plenty of courage, just like their father.

By the following morning the wind had dropped, and the river Gwendraeth was flowing quietly once again. Suddenly, Gwenllïan became aware of a new sound coming from beyond her own troops. Immediately she knew what it was: armed men on the march. It was something she'd heard many times before. When she turned her head in the direction of the sound, she was appalled to see an enormous army approaching. She was cornered. But who were these soldiers? She didn't understand. Where had they come from?

Gwenllïan didn't know that a traitor had run ahead to warn the newly landed Normans that a Welsh army was on its way to meet them. He told them to approach Kidwelly from a different direction and had led the enemy to the heart of his own people. Gwenllïan and her small band of Welsh soldiers hiding in Mynydd-y-garreg didn't stand a chance.

When she faced the enemy, Gwenllïan showed enormous courage. She did everything she could to try and drive back the enemy soldiers, but there were just too many of them.

The next part of the story is hard for me to write. With a bloodcurdling yell, one of the Normans struck Maelgwyn to the ground and he died at his mother's side. Gwenllïan was heartbroken. As she knelt to tend to her son, she too was wounded. In no time at all, she and Morgan, her other son, had been taken prisoner.

The Normans showed her no mercy. Standing next to his dead brother's body, Morgan watched in terror as the enemy leader seized Gwenllïan's golden hair and proceeded to cut off her head. She faced her death with courage, calling out 'Remember me', as the axe cut into her flesh. Her head fell to the ground, and a spring welled up on the spot. To this day the field where it happened is known as Gwenllïan's Field, Maes Gwenllïan.

What a terrible fate! Not only had she lost the battle and witnessed the killing of one of her sons, she had also forfeited her own life.

When her husband, Gruffudd, heard about the massacre, he hurried south at once. His fellow princes and the ordinary people were united in grief at Gwenllïan's death and in anger that an army of foreigners had taken the life of a princess so dear to all of them.

The Welsh couldn't forgive the Normans for their cruelty, and the fighting and bloodshed continued for many years afterwards.

So, when you are next in Kidwelly, make sure that you go and visit Maes Gwenllïan. And, as you remember Gwenllïan's bloody history, remember too how lucky we are to live in a land at peace.

Llywelyn
Our Last Prince

• • •

I bet you've never heard of me! I'm Dafydd ap Siôn from Abergwyngregyn in north Wales and I live just across the water from Puffin Island and the isle of Anglesey. It's not the sea view that makes Abergwyngregyn famous though. You may not have heard of me or where I live, but I'm sure you've heard of Llywelyn, haven't you? Llywelyn, the last prince of Wales? That's why Abergwyngregyn's so important: it's where Llywelyn had his court.

When I was growing up my best friend was Ieuan. We were allowed to go wherever we wanted, just so long as we made sure that we were back home by sunset. We'd often see Llywelyn and his men coming and going. We'd wave at them, and they'd wave back at us.

I'd first seen him when I was very much younger. Mam had taken me onto the sands when suddenly we saw a large group of men coming towards us. They were all smartly dressed but one had finer clothes than the others. He was dressed in red and gold and his wavy hair curled down to his shoulders. I asked my mother who he was. She explained that he was Prince Llywelyn. Even though I saw him lots of times after that – he even knew my name – that's my earliest memory of him.

When I got a bit older, I went to work at Llywelyn's court as an apprentice smith. My first job was to help Ifan, the blacksmith. Whenever anybody needed anything made out of metal – from a horseshoe to a sword – Ifan was the man to make it. He and I would often sit and chat by the fire. He was an old man and he could remember Llywelyn ap Gruffudd being born. He remembered making a miniature candle holder as a present for the prince's third birthday!

60

But although Llywelyn was a prince, he didn't treat his servants as servants. He treated them as if they were members of his own family. That's why everyone thought so highly of him. 'You see,' Ifan said to me one day, 'Llywelyn is a good man. Look at his home. It's not exactly a castle, is it? It doesn't need to be . . .'

'Why, Ifan?' I was curious.

'I'll tell you why. People respect him. None of us would dream of harming Llywelyn. Not for a second. We would defend him with our lives if we had to.'

'But the kings of England live in castles . . .'

'Exactly, Dafydd. Exactly. They live in castles because they don't have a choice. They always live with fear – the fear that someone will attack them. It's because their people don't respect them as we respect Llywelyn.' Ifan stoked the fire, causing a few sparks to fly. 'You see, Dafydd, Llywelyn has succeeded in bringing practically the whole of Wales under his control: nearly everyone is on his side.'

I learnt a lot from old Ifan. I loved my work and I'd have done anything for him. One day I was down by the river collecting stones to build a wall in the old smithy, when an important-looking man came up to me. I could tell that he was one of Llywelyn's men by the way he dressed.

'Hey, you, Dafydd!' he shouted. 'Leave those stones. Come over to the big field, the *cae*, tomorrow morning at six o'clock, and don't be late!' And off he went. Me? The *cae*? Six o'clock in the morning? What could he want? I told my friend Ieuan what had happened and he decided to come with me.

The sun hadn't yet risen above Penmaenmawr but the pale light was enough for us to be able to see where we were going, and so we made our way to the *cae*. When we arrived, there were around fifty boys of about our age there. I knew some of them, and some of the others had travelled from as far away as Caernarfon and Aberconwy.

Suddenly everyone fell silent. I looked up to see Llywelyn standing above us on the hillside. You could hear a pin drop: everyone wanted to hear what he had to say. 'Today we will travel together to Moel y Don.' Llywelyn's voice was strong and rang with passion. 'The time has come. Soon you will be issued with swords. You must put your trust in your leaders and follow their commands. Be strong. One for all and all for one!'

And without another word he turned on his heel and vanished. Then we received our orders: we boys were to stand behind the men. Llywelyn's brave warriors were going to be in front of us, but we'd still be facing the enemy. We were to hold our ground, whatever happened. We were all excited. And afraid too. We were going to be part of a battle, defending Gwynedd against the English. But we were only boys . . .

'Put your trust in them . . .' Llywelyn's words were spinning round in my head. I decided there and then that he wouldn't do anything to put my life in danger. After all, he knew my name, didn't he?

62

It was a four-hour walk before we finally reached the shores of the Menai Strait. The sun was high in the sky, and the headland at Moel y Don was shimmering clear below us in the heat. There were a few soldiers between us and the water, but as we looked out towards Anglesey, we could see the enemy in strength. They had built a bridge of ships which stretched from one side of the Menai Strait to the other.

I reached for my sword and saw Ieuan do the same. Neither of us said a word. We just looked over the water. We watched and waited. There were more of them than us. Had Llywelyn made a mistake? Had he brought an army of boys to fight an army of men? Would he make such a mistake? No, not the Llywelyn who knew my name. But where was he? And where was his army?

This wasn't the time to be asking questions. Suddenly I saw something flashing on the other bank. Soldiers on the move. Enemy soldiers. Shiny armour glinting in the sun, horses and foot soldiers setting off to cross the bridge . . . with only us on the other side. They were halfway across now. We were the only defence between the English army and the whole of Gwynedd. Halfway across. I gripped my sword more tightly. Halfway across . . . I tried to hide the fear that gripped my heart tighter than a blacksmith's tongs. I could see the same fear in Ieuan's eyes. For a second, my thoughts returned to the hills above Abergwyngregyn, where he and I used to play soldiers, making wooden swords and pretending to be the Welsh fighting against the English. But this wasn't make-believe. This was no laughing game. Halfway . . .

Suddenly from all around us, from the direction of Bangor and Caernarfon, I could hear the sound of horses and horseshoes, swords and shields. Hundreds and hundreds of them. Our soldiers. Our soldiers rushing towards the bridge of ships. And there, leading his men, was Llywelyn. By this time the English army had nearly reached the shore. But, rather than facing a handful of foot soldiers and fifty young boys armed only with swords, suddenly they were facing hundreds and hundreds of magnificent horses and experienced troops.

The English army started to retreat. They turned back across the bridge, back towards Anglesey. But the bridge was rocking. The ships were knocking into one another with some force. They were rolling heavily from one side to the other. Now there was a gap between the bridge and the dry land on the other side. There was no turning back. Some of the English soldiers decided to jump into the water. They preferred to try and swim back towards the Anglesey shore than face the Welsh on the mainland. Their armour was heavy. They didn't stand a chance . . .

Within half an hour, Moel y Don was deathly silent. The entire English army had disappeared without trace into the water, and their ships were like flotsam floating out towards the horizon and the setting sun.

I looked at Ieuan; Ieuan looked at me. We didn't say a word. We should have been happy, of course, but seeing so many people and horses being killed had made me go very quiet. I knew they were the enemy. I knew I was glad that they hadn't managed to cross to our side. I knew I was glad that we hadn't been killed. But they were people too. Fathers, brothers, uncles and sons. People just like us.

It was a long march home. When I got there, Mam threw her arms around me. She was so relieved.

64

'Why do they have to fight, Mam?' I asked. 'Why do they have to attack us? They say that England is a far bigger country than ours. Why can't they be satisfied with what they've got?'

For once, Mam didn't have an answer.

By the end of the month, Ieuan had become a regular soldier but I decided to stay with Ifan the blacksmith.

Abergwyngregyn was quiet. Winter came early. The first frost of December bit hard and ice slowed the river Rhaeadr Fawr on its journey towards the sea.

Just before Christmas, news reached Abergwyngregyn that Llywelyn had been killed, murdered by an Englishman. And all Llywelyn wanted was peace. He'd only fought to defend his country.

It's even colder today in Abergwyngregyn. Ieuan isn't here. There's no sign of him. I'm hoping he's alive, that he's managed to escape and is on his way home. I'd give anything to see him again. I'm sure he's on his way.

But I've got the same feeling about the English too. They'll be here soon and they'll lay claim to everything. It might be as early as tomorrow. But today I'm going for a walk. Down to the sea where I remember seeing Llywelyn for the first time. I'm going to walk to the top of the hill where Ieuan and I used to play with swords when we were lads. It will be good when he comes back. We'll have another sword fight . . . though I'm sure he'll be the victor. He's a better swordsman than me. I'm sure he'll come. Tomorrow . . .

Dafydd ab Gwilym

If you happen to be travelling along the road from Aberystwyth to Machynlleth, and you see a sign that says Penrhyn-coch, why not make a very special detour? Instead of continuing on your journey, turn off the main road, and follow the sign. When you go through Penrhyn-coch, Brogynin, you'll see another little signpost, this time with a man's name on it: 'Dafydd ap Gwilym'. Turn left at the signpost and travel along a narrow road for about a quarter of a mile. Turn left again and stop at a large slate set into the wall – on the other side you'll see the ruins of a house. That slate will tell you that this is the birthplace of one of Wales's finest poets.

Because Dafydd ap Gwilym was born over 600 years ago, we don't have any pictures of him, or a detailed record of his life, and nobody's really sure where he's buried. But let's just imagine that someone found an old manuscript amongst the ruins at Penrhyn-coch, and that it turned out to be Dafydd's life story . . .

. . . I was born in Brogynin, a region of rolling hills and winding rivers, where the sound of deer and birdsong fills the air. My mother's name was Ardudful, and my father was Gwilym Gam. I'm not quite sure how he got that name, maybe because his back was crooked or, in Welsh, '*gam*'. I don't like the name much, and that's why nowadays I prefer Dafydd ap Gwilym. I've been called Dafydd Gam a couple of times but I'm glad to say that most people know me as Dafydd ap Gwilym.

My childhood was a very happy one; there was always plenty to do: lots of trees and hills to climb, and plenty of fish to catch. One of my earliest memories is going with my parents to fish in the river by our house.

We caught a big salmon, and what a great supper we had that night!

All too soon it was time for me to leave my childhood home and go away to school, though my days with the monks at Strata Florida were very happy ones. I learnt so much there. I learnt how to read and write and how to work the land. I even learnt Latin. But although the Strata Florida monks were good teachers, the person who taught me the most was my uncle, my mother's brother, Llywelyn ap Gwilym. As constable of the castle at Newcastle Emlyn, it was his job to keep order there.

· D A F Y D D   A P   G W I L Y M ·

He lived in Dolgoch, about three miles upriver from the castle. The river Teifi. What a river! At Dolgoch, it flows quietly for a while, then crashes down over some large rocks – just like water boiling in a cauldron – before flowing gently onwards once again.

It was at Newcastle Emlyn that I got the chance to learn French, a language I thought was very beautiful. There were lots of Normans in the area, who all spoke French, of course. Some of them made an effort to learn Welsh, but others insisted that we spoke their language, so we had to learn French. We were willing to make a lot of allowances for the Normans, though, because of their wine! My uncle said that he'd never tasted anything quite so delicious.

But of all the things my uncle did for me at Newcastle Emlyn, the most important was to inspire me to become a poet. He loved words, and if I showed him some lines or verses I'd written, he'd laugh out loud. In the beginning, I thought that he was laughing at me, but after a while I realised that this was his way of showing that he liked my work. He told me all about the travelling bards who go from place to place, writing poems for important people and getting paid for it.

Getting paid for writing poems and travelling around the Welsh countryside? It sounded like heaven! From that moment onwards, I knew just what I wanted to do for a living. And so I became a poet, which gave me the opportunity to see places in Wales I'd never imagined existed.

One of the best welcomes I ever received was at Talley Abbey. In Welsh it's called Talyllychau. Tal-y-llychau. Isn't that a lovely name? I fell in love with three things:

the place, the people and the name. But I was never one to stay in the same spot for very long, no matter how warm the welcome.

I remember once my uncle telling me about a wonderful place in the very north of the country. He'd heard some poets describing it, an area where the land was more rugged, a region of mountains rather than hills. I was fascinated by the sound of it, and when I was old enough to make my own way, I decided to leave my uncle's home, and go and find it for myself. Following the sun during the daytime and the stars at night, it took me three full days to get there. I'd never seen such high mountains before. I used to think that Pumlumon was high, but there's a mountain up in the north called Snowdon and, from whichever direction you see it, it looks like a king wearing a white cap and looking down on all his lands and possessions.

But by the time I'd travelled as far as the coast, I'd left Snowdon far behind. Over the water was a flat-looking island: Anglesey, Ynys Môn. There was nothing for it but to cross the Menai Strait at Bangor and go over to Anglesey to explore. I received a very warm welcome there and even managed to visit Llanddwyn Island, a place that I'd heard a lot about. Llanddwyn is Saint Dwynwen's island, and she's the patron saint of lovers. I expect you'll have heard of my reputation with the ladies? It's true that I love female company, but if you want to know more about that, you'll have to go and read my poems!

Morfudd was one of my favourite girls. She was only eighteen years old when I saw her first, and I remember exactly where it was. I'd walked into Bangor cathedral and I was stunned by its beauty. But when I caught sight of this lovely young girl

73

about the same age as me, I forgot all about the beauty of the cathedral. Morfudd had blonde hair and black eyebrows and she was very petite. Instantly I fell head over heels in love with her. She was a long way from home, having travelled from Eithinfynydd, a farm between Llanuwchllyn and Dolgellau. Once I'd seen her, the poetry just kept flowing. Verse after verse. I couldn't stop. I had to find a way to show my love for her, and what better way than to write her a special poem? (My poems are all quite special as a matter of fact, with a particular pattern of beats and repeated sounds in each line.)

But Morfudd wasn't all sweetness and light, let me tell you. Occasionally I'd send her a message, and get nothing in return. Sometimes she'd agree to meet me, but then she'd break her promise. One time, I remember standing outside her house, waiting and waiting for her to come out. But even though I stayed there all night in the pouring rain, she didn't once come to the door. By the morning I was soaked to the skin and had to go home with a heavy heart!

The biggest disappointment of my life was when I heard that Morfudd had fallen in love with another man. Cynfrig Cynin was his real name, but I had another name for him! He and Morfudd got married and that left me lonely and unhappy. But it wasn't the end of the story though. From time to time, Morfudd and I would bump into each other, and even though she was married to somebody else I liked to think that she still preferred me!

Because I did a lot of travelling around the country, I got to stay in a whole variety of inns and boarding houses. Some really deserved to have a poem written about them,

like this one, for example. I remember arriving late at night. I had my young servant with me and the place was packed to the rafters. I decided that I wanted something to eat and, while I was trying to decide what I was going to have, suddenly I saw this girl. I'd never seen her before but she was looking at me from over the other side of the room.

Wow! She was stunning. I wanted to show her that I had really good manners and that I was a person of some importance, so I invited her over to sit with me. I bought her a meal, the finest the house could offer. I bought her the very best wine as well. I wanted that evening to go on for ever. I'd better not tell you everything that happened, but I'll tell you this much. By chasing that girl, I got into quite a scrape . . . even though I slept on my own in the end. Later on I wrote a poem about it and called it 'Trouble in a Tavern'!

On my travels around Wales, one of the places I most loved visiting was Parc Rhydderch in Ceredigion, which was the home of a man called Rhydderch, and his wife, Angharad. They always made me very welcome. Amongst the treasures they kept in their home was a very special book. It was called *The White Book of Rhydderch* and only very few people were ever allowed to write in it. It contained the lives of a number of Welsh saints, and stories from the Mabinogi, tales about Bendigeidfran and Branwen, Blodeuwedd and Gwydion. I'd read the book from cover to cover and then – I remember it as if it was yesterday – Rhydderch suddenly looked up at me, and asked me to sit in the chair in front of the fire. I wondered whether I had done something wrong. *The White Book* was open on the table at a blank page. I'll never

forget what Rhydderch said next: 'Dafydd, would you like to write one of your poems in the book?' Me? Dafydd ap Gwilym? Invited to write in *The White Book*? I couldn't believe it. What an honour for my work to appear alongside the saints' lives and those wonderful stories from the Mabinogi! I grasped the quill and started writing. Very, very carefully. My hand was shaking; I was so afraid that I'd make a mistake. At last I finished the work, and signed it. Although I wasn't too fond of my name, it was important to write it in full for this most precious of books. And so, to this day, *The White Book of Rhydderch* contains a poem by Dafydd ap Gwilym Gam.

That was one of the high points of my life but one of the saddest was when I heard that my uncle Llywelyn ap Gwilym had been killed. He was my friend and teacher as well as my uncle. But being constable of the castle was not an easy job, and he was bound to make enemies. It's strange to think that I'll never see him again, but the things he taught me and the fun that we had together will stay with me for ever.

As I'm growing older, the money that people give me for writing my poems is getting less and less. The money that I inherited from my parents is also dwindling, and I'm becoming more and more dependent upon people who are kind enough to give me board and lodging on my travels. If I see that beautiful girl in the tavern again, I don't think I'll be able to buy her as much as a cheese sandwich, let alone a roast dinner!

As I look back on my life, I'm enjoying revisiting some of the places that have meant a lot to me. I've been back to the house where I was born. Back to Talley and Strata Florida. And back to Dolgoch on the banks of the river Teifi. When I was there

with my uncle all those years ago, I could leap over the rocks from one side of the river to the other. Today I wouldn't find it so easy. Somebody would need to build a stone bridge over the river so that I could get across to the other side without having to worry about getting my feet wet!

There's only one thing that I still need to do. I've written everything that I want to write and visited everywhere that I want to visit. The only thing left is to decide where I want to be buried when my time comes. I have two places in mind. When I was a pupil with the monks at Strata Florida, I remember there was a big oak tree growing near the abbey. It was a beautiful, majestic tree, with branches reaching high up to the sky. I remember climbing that oak and I remember the view from the top: I could see for miles in every direction.

The other place I'm considering is the one with the most beautiful name in the world, Talyllychau. I'd like to think that every time people go there, they'll say the name out loud to themselves just in case they forget how beautiful it is. But I also hope that they'll say another name too, my name, remembering the happy times I spent in Talley Abbey with the monks.

Strata Florida? Talyllychau? I can't decide. Never mind: I'll think about it tomorrow.

78

Owain Glyndŵr

Let me introduce myself. My name is Crach Ffinnant. I lived in Wales many years ago – 600 to be precise – and I had a very important job. I was a bard, though some people called me a prophet, the kind of chap who can see into the future. You'd think I'd be proud of that, wouldn't you? But what makes me proudest is that I was a friend of the most amazing Welshman ever to walk this earth: Owain Glyndŵr.

Not far from Llansilin village in Powys there is a very special place called Sycharth. If you go there today, all you will see is parkland, fishponds and a large mound with trees growing all around it. But 600 years ago, this was the home of Owain and his wife and children. It was a bustling place, busy from one day's end to the next. The servants and maids got up early each morning to get everything ready. Sometimes noblemen would come from far away for a feast, and fish, meat and vegetables were always in good supply. And there was always a good supply of warmth, fun and laughter too. Marged, Owain's wife, was as hospitable as he was, and, although she had maids to help her, she always liked to take personal charge of all the preparations for any feast.

One night, after everybody had gone to bed, Owain and I were talking by the fireside, and the conversation happened to turn to some major changes that had recently started to take place in Wales. We Welshmen had begun to feel that we weren't getting a fair deal in our own country, and that everybody else was pushing us around. 'Owain, you have to do something about it,' I said.

'About what?' Owain replied.

'Well, about all these people moving into the country and thinking that they can do as they please. We need somebody to say that enough is enough. We need a leader.'

'Me? What can I do?'

I didn't say anything. I just looked at him. He didn't say anything either, just looked back. He wasn't looking at me, though; he was looking through me.

He was definitely the man for the job. He had proved himself to be an excellent soldier after many years of fighting for the English army. He'd been victorious every time. But his heart didn't lie in England, and from that night on Owain was never the same person again. There was a fire in his soul and a dream in his heart. Yes, he looked through me. But I know very well what was going through his mind. Don't forget, I've got second sight.

The wind blew cruelly through the trees in Sycharth that night and the rain drummed non-stop on the roof. But inside, it wasn't the weather that was on Owain's mind.

I know I've got the gift of being able to see into the future, but not even I thought that events would move quite so quickly. On 16 September 1400 Owain called on his family and friends to go to Glyndyfrdwy, and there in front of everyone he proclaimed himself prince of Wales. There was a crowd of over 300 people shouting and applauding the new prince! He arrived at Glyndyfrdwy known only as plain old Owain ap Gruffudd, but from that day forwards he was known as Owain Glyndŵr.

Picture the scene. There was Owain, standing on top of the hill in the sunshine, and all of his followers hanging on his every word. There was no doubt in the hearts

· OWAIN GLYNDŴR ·

of the 300 who heard him that he was the true prince of Wales. The news spread like wildfire through the nearby towns and villages, and more and more people showed their support.

One man who wasn't at all happy about this was Reginald Grey, lord of Ruthin and Dyffryn Clwyd. He was an Englishman to the core and a sworn enemy who'd tried to steal Owain's land, and so the first thing that Owain and his followers did was to go to Ruthin town and burn it to the ground.

When the king of England heard about it, he was mad with rage. What right did a Welshman have to call himself prince of Wales? Quite clearly Wales belonged to the English king, and so he sent an army to kill Owain. But the king underestimated the character of the Welsh people, and didn't realise what brave, strong fighters we are. He thought that it would be easy to conquer us, but that was not what happened. Within a few months, people all over Wales regarded Owain as their true prince.

The English king then decided on a very cruel course of action. Within a year of that announcement at Glyndyfrdwy, he decided that no Welshman should hold an important job in Wales. The Welsh weren't allowed to own any castles, not so much as a fortified manor house, and we certainly weren't allowed to carry weapons. We weren't allowed to congregate in large numbers and our poets were even forbidden to write poems in rhyme!

If the English king thought that this was the way to beat us, he was making a big mistake. Instead of making us weaker, it made us even stronger. Many people joined the campaign. Ceredigion and Powys were strong in their support for Owain, and more and more were proud to be able to say that a Welshman, Owain Glyndŵr, was the true prince of Wales.

This made the English king very, very angry and he resolved to do his utmost to kill Owain Glyndŵr and his followers. At Llandovery he decided to teach the Welsh a lesson. The English caught one of Owain's supporters, Llywelyn ap Gruffudd Fychan, and put him to a brutal death on the town square in front of the king.

The English army was stronger than the Welsh. It was bigger and had more money to buy better weapons. Yet though the English had strength on their side, the Welsh were braver and more cunning.

But Owain was in for another lesson. He had two homes, one in Glyndyfrdwy and another in Sycharth. One dark night, a troop of English soldiers went there and burnt both houses to the ground. Owain was now homeless. But there were supporters all over Wales willing to give him somewhere to shelter and to hide him from the English. If they thought that burning his houses would stop Owain from being prince of Wales, the English were badly mistaken. The war continued.

Owain hadn't forgotten about his old enemy Reginald Grey. He decided to take him prisoner and hold him captive so that the English would have to pay a ransom to get him back. One night, Owain and his men attacked Reginald Grey's home, and managed to capture him and take him to a safe place. Reginald's servants arranged to deliver the ransom money but they decided to try and trick Owain. They put fake money in a sack and took it to him. But something told Owain not to trust them. He opened the sack, poured the coins onto the table and examined them very carefully.

85

When he saw that the money was fake, he realised that the English had tried to trick him and decided to teach them a lesson in return. He sent the soldiers back to the English king, and said that if he wanted Owain to release Reginald Grey, the ransom price had now gone up! He'd have to pay twice as much.

Before long, Owain got word that a large army of English soldiers was on its way to Wales, somewhere close to where the village of Knighton lies today. On 22 June 1402 the battle of Bryn Glas took place between the Welsh and the English armies. It was a bloody battle, and both sides lost many brave soldiers. But the Welsh army won in the end, and the surviving English soldiers had to return home to their own country with their tails between their legs.

Owain's next target was Carmarthen, a town that had been ruled by the English for a very long time. The Tywi was a lovely valley, where crops grew well, the cattle grew big and fat, and where there was enough food for everybody. If he could take Carmarthen, it would strengthen Owain's position as prince of Wales. On 6 July 1403 Owain and his

86

soldiers managed to drive the English out of Carmarthen castle. Glyndŵr's banner was raised high above the walls and people from far and wide could see it waving in triumph.

By this time castles all over Wales had fallen to Owain: Newcastle Emlyn, Kidwelly, Harlech, Aberystwyth. As victory followed victory, the English got more and more angry. By the end of 1403, most people in Wales acknowledged Owain Glyndŵr as their prince. From Anglesey to Monmouth, they believed that the Welsh should rule their own country, and not have to listen to outsiders telling them what to do.

Meanwhile, the English king had problems of his own. People were plotting to get rid of him, and two of the plotters had come to an agreement with Owain. These were Henry Percy (also known as Harry Hotspur) and Edmund Mortimer, and they planned to divide Wales and England between them. There was a family connection between Edmund Mortimer and Owain because Edmund had married Owain's daughter Catrin. The three noblemen came to the small village of Bryneglwys, near Corwen, and signed an agreement, using a large flat stone as a table. From that day forth, the stone has been known as 'the table of the three lords'.

Unfortunately, neither Harry Hotspur nor Edmund Mortimer succeeded in their plot against the English king, Henry IV, and so Owain had to look for other friends in order to rule Wales with greater security. In 1404 Owain and the king of France agreed to combine forces against King Henry.

For any country to rule itself, it needs a parliament: a gathering of important people who meet to make decisions. And that's what Owain set up. He decided

87

on Machynlleth because it was right in the middle of Wales, and in 1404 he set up his parliament there. And a year later he held a parliament in Harlech.

The English campaign continued and Henry IV spent more and more of his money on weapons and horses and soldiers to try and win the war against Wales. Owain wasn't as wealthy as the English king, but he had an advantage. The Welsh soldiers knew every nook and cranny of their country, every cave and valley, every river and rock. And so, when the English army tried to beat them, the Welsh troops were always one step ahead.

But in case you think that fighting was Owain Glyndŵr's only interest, I can tell you that he was a man years ahead of his time. Once when he was in the village of Pennal, he decided to write a letter to the king of France. In this letter, he wrote about his hopes for a united Welsh church under the leadership of the Pope in Rome. He also talked about setting up a Welsh university. Owain was a thinking man as well as a man of action.

Because of my talent for predicting the future, Owain asked me many times what I thought was going to happen. At first I was able to tell him honestly that I thought we were going to win. Things were going in our favour. The majority of people in Wales were on Owain's side, and he had the support of other countries too. But little by little there was change in the air. It wasn't so much like a sudden blast of cold wind, more like a slow creeping fog. Some of the Welshmen who'd supported Owain in the past began to turn away from him. Once they heard that the English army was starting to win battles here and there, they were all too ready to turn their backs on Owain.

The worst traitor was a man called Gwilym ap Gruffudd. When Owain was at his strongest, Gwilym supported him to the hilt. He fawned over Owain like a little lapdog, but the minute things changed, Gwilym forgot his earlier loyalty, and decided to support King Henry. We don't need people like that in Wales!

In the end, there were too many turncoats like Gwilym ap Gruffudd and, in certain parts of the country, Owain found it harder and harder to keep control. The people who had once been his friends started to desert him. The English were very cunning. They offered money and promised land to anyone who supported them. The castles that Owain once controlled, Kidwelly, Aberystwyth, Harlech and Carmarthen, one by one fell into enemy hands. In spite of these setbacks, Owain was still able to create a lot of trouble for the English.

Although some Welshmen turned their backs on him, Owain didn't turn his back on Wales. The English king offered him money, a large house and land, so that he could live in comfort for the rest of his life. The only thing he had to do was bow down in front of Henry, and acknowledge him as king of Wales. Did Owain do this? No, he didn't, I'm proud to say.

I remember the last time I saw Owain Glyndŵr. The two of us had gone to Sycharth. The wind blew strongly through the trees as it had before, and a thick mist swirled. I didn't say a word; I just looked. As he gazed at the fort that was now no more than rubble, I'm sure I saw a small tear in the corner of Owain's eye. He started towards the hill and began to walk. I knew that he wanted to be on his own, that this was not the time to go after him.

This was his moment. He climbed higher and higher, and gradually disappeared into the mist.

I never saw him again. Many people have asked me where he went. They say that I, Crach Ffinnant, of all people, should know. After all, I'm the great prophet, the one who sees everything. But I don't. Not these days. However, I do know this much. Owain has left us, but not forever. When Wales needs him, really needs him, Owain Glyndŵr will return.

Twm Siôn Cati

. . .

It's a dark night with no moon and no stars. And the only sounds are the wild howling of the wind, and the rattling of the rain as it pounds the rutted highway. There are no trains, no cars – they haven't been invented yet – it's the year 1550 and all good Welsh folk are doing their best to pull the bedclothes up over their ears, praying that morning will soon come to calm the nightmare of the storm. But whilst all sensible souls are taking shelter, there's one lone vehicle out on the high road – a stagecoach – and it's carrying a handful of frightened passengers.

Oh, and there's one more person out on the road tonight, a bold Welshman hiding in the trees, watching for his opportunity. He's masked, he's holding a pistol, and he's going to give the coachman and his passengers the biggest fright of their lives. And it will be worse than any thunderstorm!

Shh! He can hear the horses' hooves getting closer. Quick as a flash, he leaps into the middle of the road. 'Stand and deliver!' he roars. 'Your money or your life!'

The travellers' worst fears have come true. It's Twm Siôn Cati and he's going to rob them of their money . . .

And for 400 years or more, Welsh storytellers have had a great time entertaining their listeners with the adventures of this famous highwayman. The best stories about him have probably been written by T. Llew Jones, the children's author. If you get the chance to read his tales of daring and danger, robbery and revenge, you won't be disappointed.

But in the meantime, let's find out more about the life and times of this surprising

94

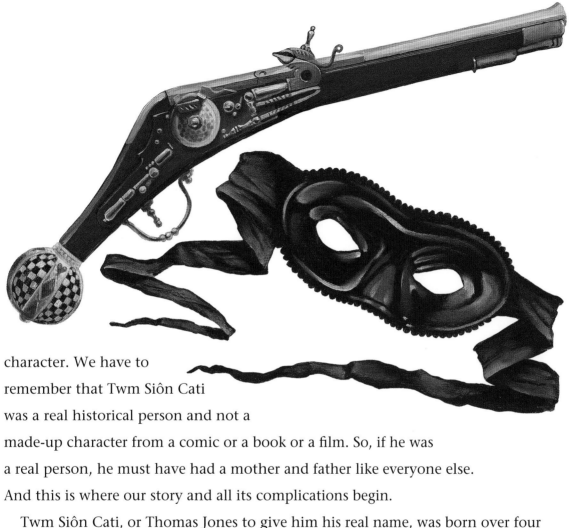

character. We have to
remember that Twm Siôn Cati
was a real historical person and not a
made-up character from a comic or a book or a film. So, if he was
a real person, he must have had a mother and father like everyone else.
And this is where our story and all its complications begin.

Twm Siôn Cati, or Thomas Jones to give him his real name, was born over four centuries ago. Nobody is really sure who his father was, but everyone thinks that he was related in some way to a leading member of the aristocracy – Sir John Wynn from Gwydir. Sir John was a very wealthy man and lived in a mansion near Llanrwst in north Wales. 'Siôn' is the Welsh form of 'John', and some say that Twm was given his middle name after Sir John. But whether this is true or not, we are fairly sure that his mother's name was Catrin. Very often 'Catrin' gets shortened to 'Cadi' or 'Cati', which explains how Twm Siôn Cati got his name: Twm, the son of John and Catrin.

Twm wasn't brought up in Llanrwst, but in Tregaron, in a house called Porth y Ffynnon (and according to some people, Twm was the illegitimate son of the local squire). Even as a young boy Twm realised how poor the ordinary people of Wales were, and how difficult it was for them to make ends meet. Even if his forefathers were landowners and didn't much care about the plight of the ordinary folk, Twm was different. He was always eager to help people . . . and some say that this is how he began his career as a lawbreaker and highwayman. Twm thought that it was unfair that some people had lots of money whilst others had nothing at all. The only answer, he decided, and the only way to make things better, was to share the country's wealth more fairly, by stealing from the rich and giving to the poor. And that is what he did.

Or at least, that's what his friends have said over the centuries. His enemies, of course, insist that he was a bad man, a criminal, and that he should have been put in prison as a common thief.

It certainly didn't take Twm very long to make enemies of the richest and most powerful people in the country. As a result, he had to go into hiding, and he spent years living in a cave near Rhandir-mwyn, not far from Tregaron. You can still see the cave today, and with a little imagination you can see why it would be a good hiding place for someone like Twm Siôn Cati. Certainly, none of the rich folk he'd offended would ever think of going there to look for him.

96

Some people say that he went into hiding not because he was a thief but because he disagreed with the queen's religious beliefs. This would have been a very risky thing to do. At that time, disagreeing with the king or queen was very dangerous – you could be hanged for it.

Let's move on quickly! I'm sure you'd prefer to hear a funny story about how Twm helped a little old lady who needed a new saucepan but didn't have enough money to buy one. This is what happened. One day, when he was out walking in the countryside, Twm saw an old woman. She was looking very worried and so he went up to talk to her. She explained that she was tired and that she was on her way to market to buy a good saucepan but that she wasn't very hopeful: she didn't have very much money and the saucepan seller was likely to charge her a high price.

'Don't you worry your head about that!' said Twm. 'I'll come with you and make sure he doesn't trick you!' And off they went on their journey.

Once they got to market, Twm and the old woman went straight over to the saucepan seller and Twm reached for the largest pan on the stall. 'Hey!' he said, brandishing the saucepan. 'This one's got a hole in it!'

'A hole?' said the pan seller in dismay. 'A hole?'

'Yes. A hole!' replied Twm.

'If you can show me the hole,' said the saucepan seller, 'I'll give you the pan for free.'

'Excellent!' said Twm, winking slyly at the old woman. She couldn't believe her ears.

Twm lifted the saucepan high into the air whilst the pan seller stared at it defiantly. 'I can't see any hole,' he declared.

And with that, Twm turned the saucepan upside down and placed it, like a hat, on the man's head. 'Well,' said Twm, 'if the saucepan didn't have a hole, you'd never have got it on your head!'

The pan seller was furious, but he had to admit that he'd lost the argument. And although it was a trick, Twm was right: there was a hole in the saucepan!

It gave Twm great pleasure to take the saucepan and present it to the old woman. She couldn't believe her luck, and thanked Twm every step of the way home for teaching the mean old pan seller a lesson.

The story about the saucepan seller is a lot nicer than some of the tales about Twm's career as a highwayman when he used to demand money from innocent travellers. But, according to legend, this handsome thief always had an eye for the ladies, and fell in love with several rich heiresses, even if it was only for the short time that he was robbing them of their money and their jewels.

As you've probably guessed by now, Twm wasn't always lucky and, like most criminals in the end, he got caught. To avoid going to prison, or even worse, being put to death, he escaped to Geneva in Switzerland. But after a couple of years he was granted a royal pardon and was able to return to Wales a free man.

It seems that one of the first things he did on coming home was to marry Siwan, or Joan, the daughter of Sir John Price of Montgomeryshire, the widow of the Sheriff of Carmarthen. She was a very wealthy woman, and, by marrying her, Twm Siôn Cati became a respectable gentleman. He even got to sit in court as a justice of the peace, punishing criminals and sending them to prison!

99

He spent much of his time after that researching the history of large Cardiganshire families, and earning quite a bit of money. At that time, many people wanted to be able to say that they were related to someone 'important', and they were prepared to pay good money to any historian who could trace their family back to some prince or other . . . and Twm was just the man for the job: he certainly had enough imagination!

Some say that Twm wrote poetry – and even that he won a chair in an important eisteddfod. According to Dr John David Rhys, who lived at about the same time, Twm was the most famous and talented poet of his day. They say that his poems can still be found in the British Museum in London . . .

Nobody will ever know the exact truth about Twm Siôn Cati, but we can all enjoy the stories about this colourful character, even if we have to take them with a very large pinch of salt! One thing's certain: it's a lot nicer to think of him as a man who believed in fair shares for all than a cold-hearted thief who went about terrorising innocent people.

But when howling winds and pelting rain turn midnight dreams to nightmare, you can sometimes imagine the sound of hoof beats coming closer and a man's voice calling: 'Your money or your life!'

That's when it's good to know that Twm Siôn Cati's adventures belong to the past and that nobody, not even the reader of this story, has anything to fear!

100

Guto Nyth Brân

You've seen Olympic sprinters
Who move at the speed of light
But here's a boy with the wind at his heels
And the grace of an eagle's flight.

No other runner could catch him,
Not a boy, but a lightning streak,
And he'd clear every obstacle in his path
As he raced to the mountain peak.

Guto Nyth Brân,
His soul on fire
With love for Siân,
His heart's desire.

Not a creature could outrun him,
Not even the swiftest hare,
And neither dog nor stallion
Could with his speed compare.

104

So fleet of foot was Guto
The sheep came to his call,
Before his father blinked an eye
He'd lured and penned them all.

When running teatime errands
Guto really showed his mettle,
For he'd be home before his mam
Had time to boil the kettle.

Guto Nyth Brân,
His soul on fire
With love for Siân,
His heart's desire.

Now Guto was a boy whose speed
Is celebrated still
And men turned pennies into pounds
By betting on his skill.

A challenger arrived – John Prince –
Whose horse won all its races.
'I know we'll beat the lad,' he jeered.
'Let's put him through his paces.'

But Guto liked a challenge
And he slept a dreamless sleep,
His rival's boasts could not disturb
A confidence so deep.

Throughout the night he dreamt that he
And Siân together lay,
Her body nestled in his arms
Beneath a quilt of hay.

Next day he jogged his way to town
Appearing in no hurry,
Despite the crowd's excitement
He knew he needn't worry.

'Get going, Guto!' roared the throng,
'For Prince and his horse are flying,
Siân's the prize you're going to lose,
And clearly you're not trying.'

But Guto knew that at the start
He shouldn't run too fast.
To win a steeplechase like this
His strength would need to last.

How right he was, for mile by mile
The horse began to tire,
Whilst Guto's stamina increased
With every passing spire.

He bounded like a year-old stag,
All obstacles he cleared,
He kept his eyes fixed straight ahead
As the finishing post he neared.

With Newport far behind him
And Bedwas next in sight,
A little church and journey's end
Filled Guto with delight.

And as he crossed the finishing line
The crowd all cheered, 'Hurray!
All honour to our champion,
For Guto's won the day.'

Guto Nyth Brân,
His soul on fire
With love for Siân,
His heart's desire.

He stepped towards his darling girl
For a longed-for lover's greeting.
'Well done!' said Siân, and clasped him close:
With that, his heart stopped beating.

The race it ended with the day

And with the winner's death,

That mountain runner swift as thought

Had breathed his final breath.

No winner's purse could comfort her,

His broken-hearted Siân,

For she had valued nothing more

Than the love of Guto Nyth Brân.

First published in Wales in 2012 by Pont Books, an imprint of
Gomer Press, Llandysul, Ceredigion, SA44 4JL
www.gomer.co.uk

ISBN 978 1 84851 474 4

A CIP record for this title is available from the British Library.

This book is based on *Trysorfa Arwyr Cymru*, an original work by Tudur Dylan Jones.

This book is published with the financial support of the Welsh Books Council.

Printed and bound in Wales at
Gomer Press, Llandysul, Ceredigion.